For Emily

Callahans
Christmas 1988

D0538362

The Tigers Brought Pink Lemonade

Poems by Patricia Hubbell   Illustrations by Ju-Hong Chen

ATHENEUM   1988   NEW YORK

For Hal
P. H.

To Mi Le
J-H.C.

Text copyright © 1988 by Patricia Hubbell
Illustrations copyright © 1988 by Ju-Hong Chen

Atheneum
Macmillan Publishing Company
866 Third Avenue, New York, NY 10022
Collier Macmillan Canada, Inc.

Type set by V & M Graphics, New York City
Printed and bound in Japan
Typography by Mary Ahern
First Edition

10 9 8 7 6 5 4 3 2 1

Library of Congress Cataloging-in-Publication Data

Hubbell, Patricia.
The tigers brought pink lemonade: poems/by Patricia Hubbell;
illustrations by Ju-Hong Chen. —1st ed.
p.   cm.
Summary: Poems, mostly about animals, some fantastic, some
humorous, with such titles as "Questions for a Dinosaur" and "A
Snail's Needs Are Very Small."
ISBN 0–689–31417–5
1. Children's poetry, American. [1. American poetry.
2. Humorous poetry. 3. Animals—Poetry.] I. Chen, Ju-Hong, ill.
II. Title.
PS3558.U22T5   1988
811'.54—dc 19
87–27800 CIP AC

CONTENTS

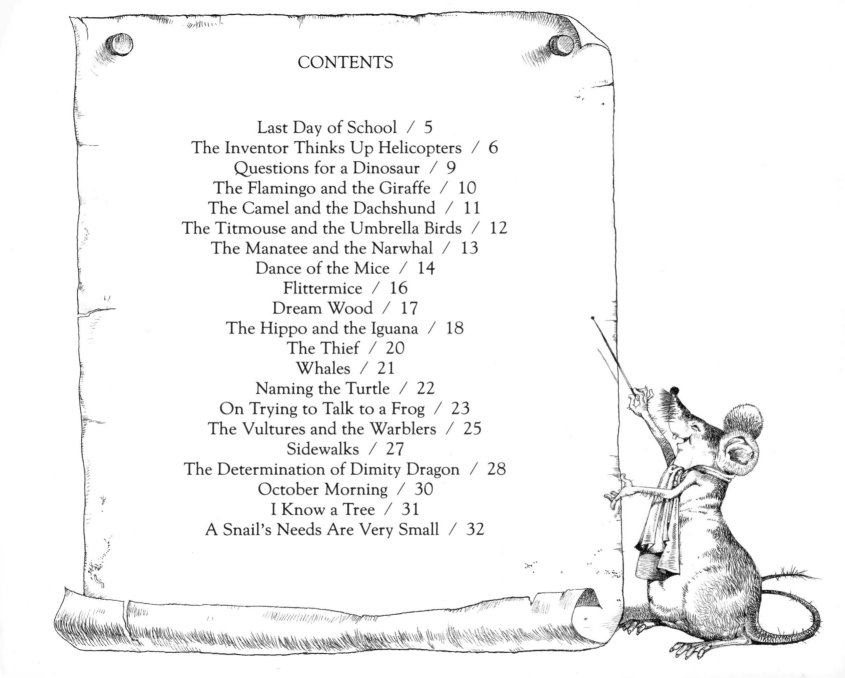

LAST DAY OF SCHOOL

*T*his morning, the pigeons were dancing through hoops
    And the world was a circus parade—
I rode my white elephant down through the town
    And the tigers brought pink lemonade.

They batted their paws,
    they roared and they cheered,
      Did somersaults,
        side-flips and twirls,

As I rode my white elephant
down through the town
When the world was a circus parade.

5

THE INVENTOR THINKS UP HELICOPTERS

"*W*hy not
a
vertical
whirling
winding
bug,
that hops like a cricket
crossing a rug,
that swerves like a dragonfly
testing his steering,
twisting and veering?
Fleet as a beetle.
Up
down
left
right,
jounce, bounce, day and night.
It could land in a pasture the size of a dot . . .
Why not?"

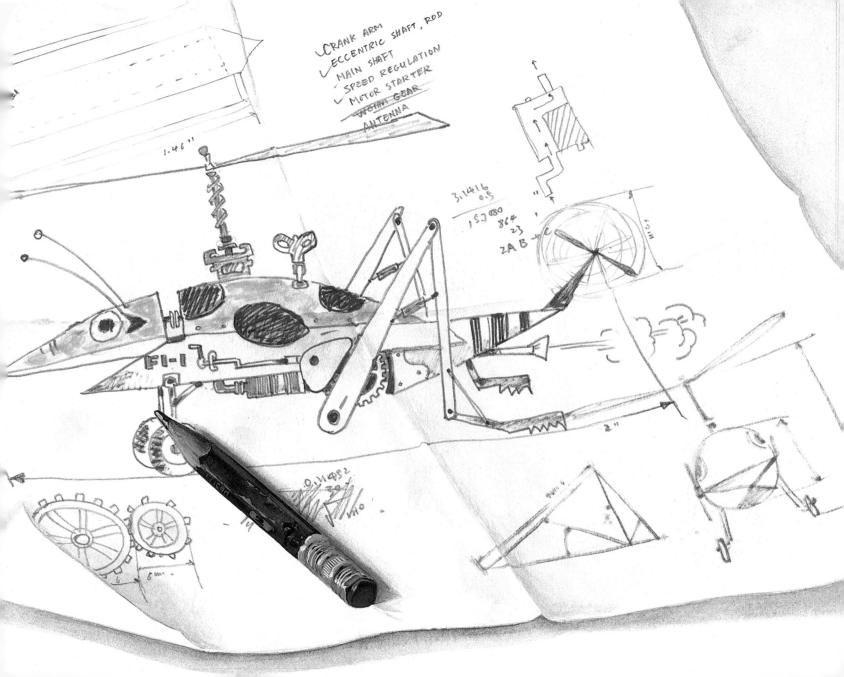

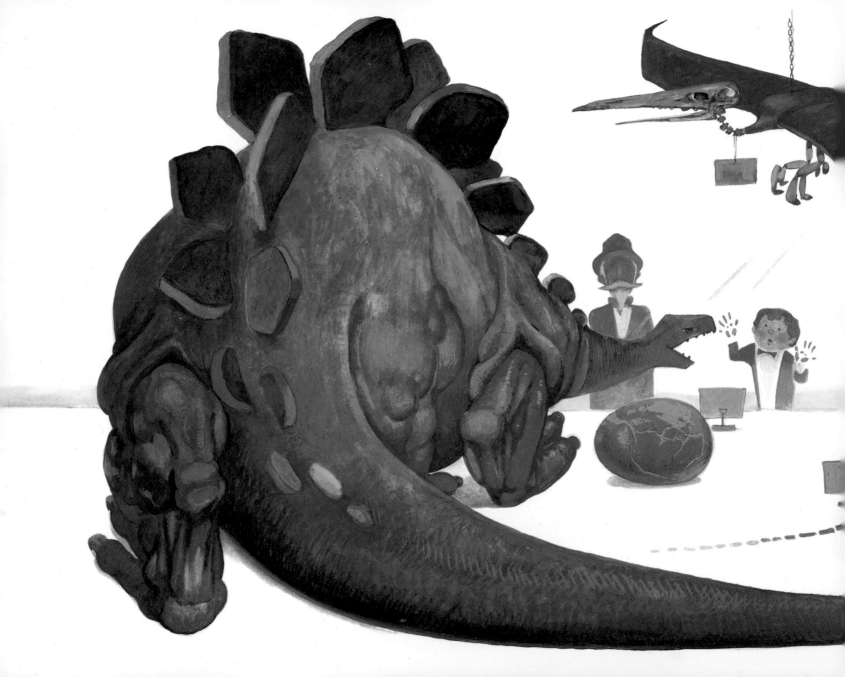

QUESTIONS FOR A DINOSAUR

O Stegosaurus,
  if you saw us,
  would you be
  against or for us?

Would you shout,
  "Hooray, we're linked!"
  Or would you wish
  we were extinct?

THE FLAMINGO AND THE GIRAFFE

A Flamingo and a young Giraffe
went stepping out one day—
  Their necks—so long,
  Their legs—so slim,
  Their heads—up in the trees—
  (A certain similarity
  extends down to their knees.)
Said Flamingo to Giraffe: "I wish
  that we might never part."
Giraffe replied: "I know. I know.
  You've won my aching heart."
So now, forever, side by side,
they stroll about the earth,
high-minded, full of high ideals,
and happy at their hearth.

THE CAMEL AND THE DACHSHUND

Said the Camel to the Dachshund:
"You have lots of room for humps.
How is it that your back's so straight—
Just smoothness—with no bumps?"

Said Dachshund to the Camel:
"I have room for humps, that's true.
But think of this—If I had humps,
Then who would admire *you?*"

11

THE TITMOUSE AND THE UMBRELLA BIRDS

An Umbrella Bird sang in his bower
while taking his midmorning shower—
He trilled to his mate:
"This umbrella is great—
It keeps me so dry when I shower!"

A Titmouse (on tour of the Andes)
Spotted the Birds and cried: "Grand! These
Birds are so rare—
Still, I've spotted a pair
as they shower in their bower—and they're dandies!"

THE MANATEE AND THE NARWHAL

The arctic Narwhal seldom sees
the tropic Manatee.
But once (by chance and fate) two met
in the vast Sargasso Sea.
This warm, weed-woven land had lured
the Narwhal from his ice.
Likewise, it called the Manatee
from her tropic paradise.
They met. They loved. They floated free—
comrades in the weeds—
the Narwhal with his spiraled beak,
the pleasant Manatee.

Now they winter in Miami,
spend summers on the floes—
(The Narwhal loves the palm trees;
Manatee loves the snows.)
Content (in spite of differences)
two mammals of the sea—
Each spring, the vast Sargasso hosts
their anniversary.

DANCE OF THE MICE

Down the runnels
and the tunnels
in the sea-grass
and the weeds
when night and purple ocean
sift among the flowing reeds
there's a shifting
and a shaking
of green blades
above the sand
as the mice come exploring
in a huge, gray band.

By hundreds,
  by thousands,
    they swarm beneath the moon—
      they are streaming
        from the rushes,
          they are pouring
            down the dune.
          They have formed a magic circle
          in the center of the sand
          and each mouse
        is swiftly waltzing   a shaking golden river
      to a tune   quivers down the dune
that rocks the beach   how they whirl! how they twirl!
Faster now   how they caper and cavort
and faster!   their tails
Every eye   are silver lashes
a little moon—   their whiskers
                                                       silver threads
                                                     and the beach is silver-flooded
                                                   flooded gold beneath the moon
                                                 as the mice
                                               go midnight dancing
                                             to the waves'
                                           hypnotic tune.

FLITTERMICE

*O*n leathery wings, the flittermice fly
　　across the starry August sky.
I watch from my porch as they wheel by.

They rush in a stream through the hay-mow door
　　of the old red barn near the sycamore,
to skim the pines and loop and soar.

Like little witches, they dodge and soar,
　　then circle the sycamore tree once more.
Four swerve back, through the wide barn door.

I watch the flittermice glide and swing
　　across the sky in their magic ring
and wonder how anything

wild as that
could ever be called by the plain name: "Bat."

DREAM WOOD

𝒦angaroos
hop
in the woods of my dream:

(Owl presents them:
bone of mice
drift of feather
tuft of fur
scent of mole
scent of weasel)

(Their babies
curl to sleep
in pockets
soft as night)

Owl croons them sleepy:
    "Kaa . . . rooo
    Kaa . . . roooo
    Kaa . . . rooooo"

17

THE HIPPO AND THE IGUANA

*A*n Iguana
from Botswana
met a Hippo
from Peru.
Said Iguana:
"Are you lonesome?
Is there something I can do?"
Replied Hippo:
"I'm not lonesome,
but I *am* a bit confused—
If you would, my dear Iguana,
would you tell me—Is it true—
Shouldn't *I* be from Botswana?
Shouldn't *you* be from Peru?"

THE THIEF

I took a picnic
  to the beach.
    I packed one sandwich
      and a peach.

As I was sitting
  down to eat,
    a seagull landed
      at my feet.

With one swift leap
  he pecked my peach
    and packed my sandwich
      down
              the
                    beach.

20

WHALES

*W*hales are passing,
a pod of whales,
tail to snout.
They roll and arc
like waves riding upon waves.
They wear white lilies
in their blowholes.
The sun shivers
as they billow past.
I strain to hear their songs,
but the wind's fat fingers
plug my ears.

NAMING THE TURTLE

Slowpod,
Weightlifter,
Housemover,
Homelover.

Seaflipper,
Rainstopper,
Pond-land-
    and-stream-dweller.

Platepacker,
Boneback,
Hardshell
and Softhat.

Clicktoe
and Stare-eye,
Budhead
and Stemneck.

Nob-bob and
Lookslow,
Spotback
and Ridgetop.

Plod-plod
and Plopplop,

Logloving
Rockstone.

ON TRYING TO TALK TO A FROG

"Hey!
  greenglove
  O slicksleeve!

stir-stump
my wet-skin,
my grabgnat, my
tape-tongue—

swim fast
my muck-love,
my leap-boy,
my . . . "

        "Brrump. Brruump. Brruuump."

THE VULTURES AND THE WARBLERS

*W*arblers warble. Vultures don't.
Vultures shriek, but warblers won't.

Warblers eat their sweetmeats neatly.
Vultures gobble prey completely.

Warblers flit through sunlit boughs.
Vultures perch on skulls of cows.

Warblers win admiring glances.
Vultures have to take their chances.

SIDEWALKS

A sidewalk is a wide walk
  A let's-step-out-and-stride-walk
    A two-abreast-let's-glide-walk
      An arm-in-arm-let's-talk-walk
        A pigeon-and-a-bug-walk
          A shoulder-hugging-snug-walk
          A hot-dog-and-balloon-walk
        An under-sun-or-moon-walk
      A grass-grows-in-the-crack-walk
    A rainy-day-wet-track-walk
  A place where you and I walk
And talk and talk and talk.

THE DETERMINATION
OF DIMITY DRAGON

*D*imity Dragon faced disgrace—
She wouldn't go up to wash her face.
Her mama pleaded. Her papa cajoled.
Said stubborn Dimity:
"I'm too old.
I'm thirty thousand years plus two.
I will not wash my face for you."

Her papa begged. Her mama ranted.
Stubborn Dimity's feet stayed planted.

OCTOBER MORNING

It's an apple-dumpling dandy day—
The gray mouse scampers through the hay,
Oak trees feel their crisp leaves curl,
Maples leap and twirl.

Now fields are singing songs to fall,
And earth pulls on October's shawl.
In every bush, birds shout "Hooray!"
This apple-dumpling dandy day.

I KNOW A TREE

I know a tree that blooms at night
with blossoms of gold edged in malachite.

Its odor is nothing like anything other
than tulips in jam or incense in clover.

Its leaves are flashes of silver-gleam.
The veins are ivory. The stems are cream.

The trunk of the tree is slim and sleek,
its wood has the glow of polished teak.

Its roots are tangled and dense and gray
with delicate globules of pale Tokay—

I taste its fruit—so fine, so few—
Roses in raindrops, daisies in dew.

31

A SNAIL'S NEEDS ARE VERY SMALL

Sea-foam,
wet stone,
shell home.

These three
please me
mightily.